A IS FOR APPLE

THERE THEY ARE!!!
DID YOU SPOT THEM?

B IS FOR BAT

I SPY WITH MY LITTLE EYE SOMETHING THAT GOES HOOT!

AN OWL GOES HOOT!

C IS FOR CAT

I SPY WITH MY LITTLE EYE
3 GHOSTS

D IS FOR DEVIL

I SPY WITH MY LITTLE EYE 5 EYE BALLS

E IS FOR EYEBALL

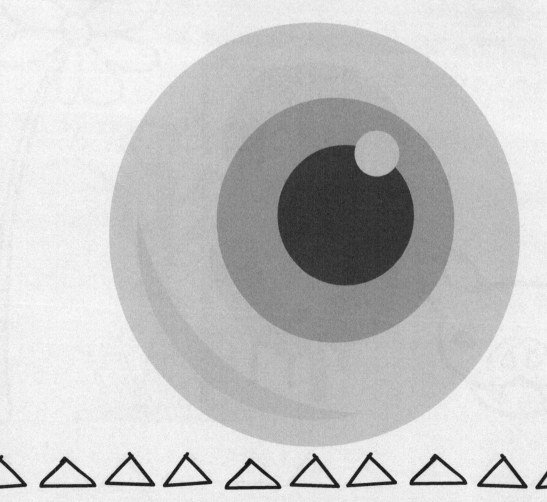

A MOUSE GOES SQUEAK!

I SPY WITH MY LITTLE EYE SOMETHING BEGINNING WITH...

F IS FOR FROG

I SPY WITH MY LITTLE EYE
2 SKELETONS

THERE THEY ARE!
DID YOU SPOT THEM?

I SPY WITH MY LITTLE EYE SOMETHING BEGINNING WITH...

G IS FOR GRAYESTONE

I SPY WITH MY LITTLE EYE 6 LOLLIPOPS

H IS FOR
HAUNTED
HOUSE

A GHOST GOES BOOOO!

I SPY WITH MY LITTLE EYE SOMETHING BEGINNING WITH...

THERE THEY ARE!
DID YOU SPOT THEM?

I SPY WITH MY LITTLE EYE SOMETHING BEGINNING WITH...

J IS FOR
JACK O
LANTERN

I SPY WITH MY LITTLE EYE 3 OWLS

THERE THEY ARE!!!
DID YOU SPOT THEM?

K IS FOR KEY

A CAT GOES MEOOW!

I SPY WITH MY LITTLE EYE SOMETHING BEGINNING WITH...

L IS FOR LEAF

THERE THEY ARE!
DID YOU SPOT THEM?

I SPY WITH MY LITTLE EYE SOMETHING BEGINNING WITH...

M IS FOR MUMMY

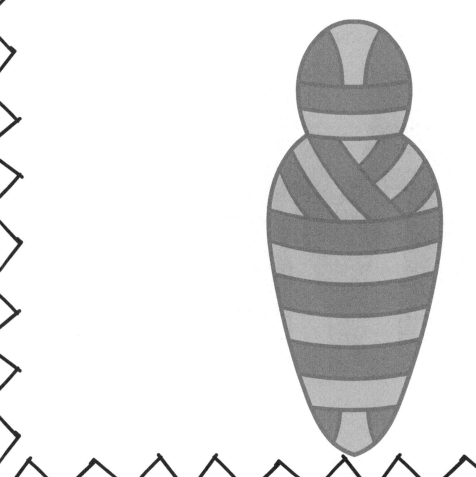

I SPY WITH MY LITTLE EYE 3 FALL LEAVES

I SPY WITH MY LITTLE EYE SOMETHING BEGINNING WITH...

N IS FOR NEST

I SPY WITH MY LITTLE EYE SOMETHING BEGINNING WITH...

O IS FOR ORANGE

I SPY WITH MY LITTLE EYE
3 TREES

THERE THEY ARE!
DID YOU SPOT THEM?

I SPY WITH MY LITTLE EYE SOMETHING BEGINNING WITH...

P IS FOR POTION

I SPY WITH MY LITTLE EYE 7 APPLES

Q IS FOR QUEEN

A LION GOES RAWR!

R IS FOR ROBOT

I SPY WITH MY LITTLE EYE
4 BALLOONS

THERE THEY ARE!
DID YOU SPOT THEM?

S IS FOR SPIDER

I SPY WITH MY LITTLE EYE 3 BUGS

THERE THEY ARE!!! DID YOU SPOT THEM?

I SPY WITH MY LITTLE EYE SOMETHING BEGINNING WITH...

T IS FOR TRICK OR TREAT

I SPY WITH MY LITTLE EYE SOMETHING THAT GOES QUACK!

I SPY WITH MY LITTLE EYE SOMETHING BEGINNING WITH...

U

U IS FOR UMBRELLA

I SPY WITH MY LITTLE EYE
6 MUSHROOMS

V IS FOR VAMPIRE

THERE THEY ARE! DID YOU SPOT THEM ALL?

I SPY WITH MY LITTLE EYE SOMETHING BEGINNING WITH...

W IS FOR WITCH

X IS FOR XYLOPHONE

I SPY WITH MY LITTLE EYE SOMETHING BEGINNING WITH...

Y IS FOR YOYO

I SPY WITH MY LITTLE EYE SOMETHING BEGINNING WITH...

Z IS FOR ZOMBIE

Well Done You Have Finished!

Don't forget to ask for the next books in the series by searching "Clever Owl Publishing" over on Amazon

We specialize in creating personalized books for kids and adults of all ages and for all occasions. We create a variety of interactive books such as Birthday Activity and Affirmation books to Gratitude and Prompted Journals.

Our books will help you to show your appreciation for the very special people in your life.

Made in United States
North Haven, CT
11 October 2021